Po's Two Dads

adapted by Erica David

Ready-to-Read

Simon Spotlight

New York   London   Toronto   Sydney   New Delhi

SIMON SPOTLIGHT
An imprint of Simon & Schuster Children's Publishing Division
1230 Avenue of the Americas, New York, New York 10020
This Simon Spotlight edition December 2015

For information about special discounts for bulk purchases, please contact Simon & Schuster Special Sales at
1-866-506-1949 or business@simonandschuster.com.
Manufactured in the United States of America 1115 LAK
2 4 6 8 10 9 7 5 3 1
ISBN 978-1-4814-4108-7 (hc)
ISBN 978-1-4814-4107-0 (pbk)
ISBN 978-1-4814-4109-4 (eBook)

Many years ago, when he was a cub,
Po was adopted by Mr. Ping.
Po loved his dad very much.
And Mr. Ping loved his son.
He was always proud of Po,
even before Po became the
Dragon Warrior.

One day a hungry stranger came to Mr. Ping's noodle shop.

"Who's eating my dumplings?" asked Po.

"And who's paying for them?" added Mr. Ping.

"I'm Li Shan," said the stranger. "I'm looking for my son."

Po and Li had the same face,
the same feet, and the same
big belly that jiggled.
Li was Po's long-lost panda dad.
"This is amazing!" said Po.

Po took Li to the Hall of Heroes
at the Jade Palace.
"This place is . . . ," Li began.
"Awesome?" finished Po.
"You were going to say awesome
because it totally is!"

Po and Li played with all the
priceless kung fu treasures
and armor.
Li even tried on the armor.
"I'm going to get you!" he teased,
chasing Po.

Li said he lived in
a secret Panda Village.
He asked Po to go there with him.
"You can learn to live
like a panda," Li said.
"And I can teach you
the power of chi."

Chi is the energy that flows
through all living things.
According to the scrolls,
Po needed to learn about
chi in order to defeat
an evil kung fu master
named Kai.

Mr. Ping was worried that
Li would take Po away forever.
So he snuck into Po's travel bag
and went with them to the
Panda Village.
When Li and Po arrived,
everyone welcomed Po!

The pandas taught Po
how to live like a panda.
First they taught him how
pandas go uphill by catapulting
on bamboo trees!
No more stairs!

Then they taught him how
pandas go downhill.
"Pandas don't walk.
We roll!" Li pointed out.

They taught him to play games like a panda.

They taught him to ribbon
dance like a panda.

And they taught him to eat
like a panda.
Why eat one dumpling
with chopsticks when you
can eat ten with your hands?

Li showed Po a picture
from when he was a baby.
Po felt like the panda
he was meant to be!

Meanwhile Mr. Ping felt left out.
Po was too busy to eat his dumplings.
But then something wonderful
happened.
The other pandas in the village
discovered what a good cook he was.
They couldn't get enough
of Mr. Ping's food!

The next day Po's friend
Tigress arrived.
She told Po that Kai
was coming to attack
the Panda Village!
It was up to Po to save it!

Po was ready to learn about chi
to save the village.
"Show me now, Dad," Po said.
But Li looked sad. He had lied to Po.
He didn't know anything about chi.
"I didn't want to lose you,"
he told Po.

Po had no other choice.
He had to teach the pandas
how to fight.
He would use the skills
they already had!
When Kai attacked,
the pandas could bounce, play,
hug, and twirl their way to victory!

Mr. Ping knew that he and Li had something in common. They both loved Po, and they didn't want to lose him. "Having you in Po's life doesn't mean less for me. It means more for Po," Mr. Ping told Li.

Mr. Ping and Li decided
to work together.
The village was in danger,
and Po needed both his dads!
So when Kai and his army came,
Po's two dads fought together
as a team.

Soon the battle came down
to Po and Kai.
Po tried a special kung fu
finger hold on Kai,
but it didn't work.
Kai was too powerful!

Po would have to try something else.
He did the finger hold on himself,
and the two warriors blasted off
into the Spirit Realm.

But Po was still losing.
He needed help.
Back in the village,
Li had a bright idea.
He gathered the pandas together.
And Mr. Ping too.
They lent their chi to Po!
In the Spirit Realm, Po saw their
chi in the form of golden paw prints.

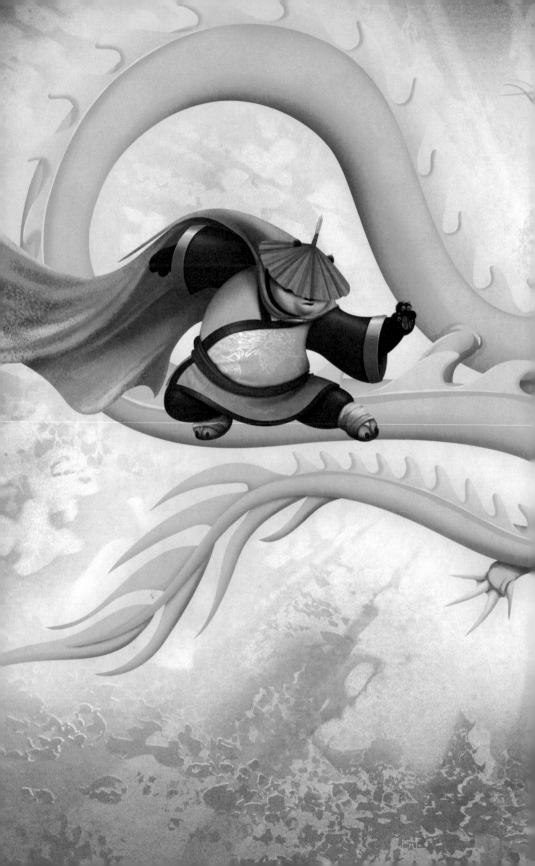

With more chi power,
Po could unleash his inner dragon.
After all, he was the Dragon Warrior!
Po won!

Po returned from the Spirit Realm.
He hugged his dads
and thanked both of them
for helping him defeat Kai.
Together they had saved
all of China.

Soon after the battle,
Po and Mr. Ping welcomed
Li and all the pandas
to their new home
in the Valley of Peace.
Po taught them kung fu.

And Po spent time with both
his dads.
He felt like the luckiest son
in the world.